A Surprise Halloween Costume

"Are you really going to wear pajamas for Halloween?" asked a boy named Danny who was sitting with Russell and Jeremy at the lunch table.

"No," said Russell. "I'm not wearing pajamas and I'm not going to be a tiger. I have a new costume."

"What is it?" asked Jeremy.

"It's a surprise."

"Is it a robot?" asked Danny.

"No."

"Is it a monster?" asked Jeremy.

"No."

"Tell me," Jeremy begged. "I told you what I'm going to be."

"It's a surprise," Russell said. "You have to wait till Halloween to find out."

Read all the books about
Nora, Teddy, Russell, and Elisa

J

Johanna Hurwitz

Russell Sprouts

illustrated by Debbie Tilley

HarperTrophy®
An Imprint of HarperCollinsPublishers

To two of my favorite Michaels,
Michael Clive and Michael Morris,
with love

Harper Trophy® is a registered trademark of
HarperCollins Publishers Inc.

Russell Sprouts
Text copyright © 1987 by Johanna Hurwitz
Illustrations copyright © 2001 by Debbie Tilley
For information address HarperCollins Children's Books, a division of
HarperCollins Publishers,
1350 Avenue of the Americas, New York, NY 10019.

Library of Congress Cataloging-in-Publication Data
Hurwitz, Johanna.
    Russell sprouts / Johanna Hurwitz ; illustrated by Debbie Tilley.
        p.   cm.
    Summary: First grader Russell Michaels grows more than an inch taller, becom-
ing big enough to wear his red slicker and big enough to deal with family and
school challenges.
    ISBN 0-06-442144-9 (pbk.)
    [1. Growth—Fiction. 2. Schools—Fiction. 3. Family life—Fiction.] I. Tilley,
Debbie, ill. II. Title.
PZ7.H9574 Ru   2001   00-039676
[Fic]—dc21   CIP
                                                                     AC

First Harper Trophy edition, 2001
❖
Visit us on the World Wide Web!
www.harperchildrens.com

Contents

The Hand-Me-Up

Russell Michaels was six years old. His home was an apartment building in New York City. The best thing about living in an apartment building was that his best friend, Teddy, lived there, too. Russell lived on the second floor with his parents and his little sister, Elisa. Teddy lived with his parents and his big sister, Nora, on the seventh floor. Teddy was seven, a year older than Russell. Sometimes Russell wished he were just the same age as Teddy. But most of the time, he was glad to be the age and size that he was. It made him proud to have an older friend in second grade.

About twice a year, Teddy's mother would sort through all his clothing and set aside everything that was too small for Teddy. Then she would put the outgrown but not worn-out clothes into a big shopping bag or a box and bring them downstairs to the second floor for Russell. If something was too small for Teddy, it was likely that it was just the right size for Russell.

The night before, after Russell was asleep, Teddy's mother had brought a big box of Teddy's outgrown clothes down to Russell's apartment.

"Hand-me-downs!" said Russell's mother with delight when she showed the box to Russell the next day.

"If we lived upstairs over Teddy instead of downstairs below him, would these be hand-me-ups?" Russell wanted to know.

Mrs. Michaels laughed. "I never thought of it that way, but I guess they would," she agreed. She took everything out of the box and held each piece of clothing up against Russell.

There was the winter coat with toggles that Teddy had worn last year. There was a T-shirt with a picture of Mickey Mouse and another one with a picture of Superman. Teddy had neat clothes and Russell was glad that he could wear them.

"It's too bad that we can't give any clothing to Teddy in return," said Mrs. Michaels.

Russell laughed. It was a funny thought. If *he* was too big for his old jacket and pants, then Teddy would certainly be too big. So some of Russell's old clothing was put away for Elisa to grow into. Elisa was only three years old, but when she got bigger she could wear lots of his outgrown clothes, including his old yellow rain slicker.

Russell was glad that his slicker didn't fit him any more. He wanted to get a new one that was red because red was his favorite color. His favorite toy cars were red and his bike was red, too. He even liked to eat red things like spaghetti with lots of tomato sauce or hamburgers with loads of catsup.

Mrs. Michaels took Russell shopping for a new red slicker. They went to four different stores, but they couldn't find a red one.

"How about blue?" Mrs. Michaels asked finally.

"No," said Russell. "I want red."

"Yellow is a very popular color," said the saleswoman.

"No," said Russell.

Mrs. Michaels sighed. "Next week we'll go to some other stores," she promised. "But if we can't find a red one, I'm afraid you'll have to settle for another color."

Then something wonderful-awful happened. Russell's grandmother saw a red slicker in the children's department of a store near her home. She knew that Russell liked red things the best. So when she saw the red slicker, she bought it for him and put it in a package and mailed it to Russell.

When the package arrived, Russell was

very excited. He usually received packages when it was his birthday, which was in the spring. But this was September, and his birthday wasn't going to come around again for months and months. The red slicker was just the way Russell imagined it. At least that's the way it looked until he tried it on. The coat came down almost to his ankles and the sleeves were so long that his hands were hidden.

"Oh, Russell. This is much too big," said his mother, laughing. "We'll just have to ask Grandma to return it."

"No, no," shouted Russell. "I like it big. It will keep me extra dry."

"You won't be able to move in it," said his mother. "It is really a shame, but you look a little like a circus clown."

"No, I don't," Russell protested. But when he peeked in the bathroom mirror,

he saw that he did look pretty silly in this too-big slicker.

"I'm growing," said Russell hopefully. "You said I was growing so much. I bet it will fit me next week. Please, can't I keep it?"

Mrs. Michaels sighed. "I guess we can keep it," she said. "But I'll still have to get you a new slicker to wear this season. Unless, of course, you inherit something from Teddy."

Then Mrs. Michaels smiled. "You know," she said, "this red slicker would probably fit Teddy right now. I think we should let him wear it until you grow into it."

"Teddy can't have it," Russell protested. He wanted to keep the slicker in his closet. "It's mine!"

"Russell, that's being selfish," said his mother. "Think how many clothes you've gotten from Teddy over the years." She pointed to the red-and-white-striped shirt that Russell was wearing at that very moment. It used to belong to Teddy.

"But I want to be able to look at my red slicker," Russell complained.

"You'll be able to look at it on Teddy," said his mother. "And I promise you, before you know it, you'll be wearing it yourself and he'll be looking at it on you."

So that was how Teddy Resnick became the temporary owner of a bright new red rain slicker and why Russell Michaels was seen walking to school on rainy days in an old yellow one. Russell was wearing a hand-me-down from Teddy and for once Teddy was wearing a hand-me-up from Russell.

Bad Words

Now that Russell Michaels was six years old, he was in first grade. His mother had bought him a lunch box last year when he was in kindergarten. This year he had a knapsack, too. In it he carried his notebook and his reader. Often, when he returned from school, his knapsack was filled with worksheets that he had completed in the classroom. At home the refrigerator was covered with the pages that Russell had done. They all were marked with bright red checks and messages from Mrs. Evans, his teacher.

Some papers said "Good Work." Other papers said "Excellent." Russell was proud of all his good papers and the praise from his teacher. They proved that he was learning a lot of new things at school. Soon he would know how to write everything in the world, and he would be able to read, too.

But one day Russell brought something home with him that he didn't carry inside his knapsack or inside his lunch box. He carried it inside his head. It was discovered when Russell came home from school and saw that his little sister, Elisa, had been playing with his toy cars while he was away. Russell shouted at Elisa, and he used a word that made his mother angry with him.

"That was a bad word," she said. "We don't use that word in this family."

Russell was so surprised that for a moment he forgot his anger. "How can a word be bad?" he asked, puzzled.

"Some words are not nice for people to use," his mother explained. "They are very rude."

Russell whispered the word under his breath. It didn't sound bad or rude to him. He couldn't even remember where he had learned it. All the words he knew were just floating around inside his head. He couldn't help it if his mother didn't like that word. He did.

Russell said the bad word aloud again.

"No, Russell," his mother scolded. "I told you that I don't want to hear you using that word any more!"

Elisa repeated the bad word that Russell had said. Russell laughed. "See," he told his mother. "Elisa likes that word, too."

"Elisa just learned that word from you. And you must have learned it from someone at school. But that doesn't make it right. I don't want you to say it again. If you are feeling angry, there are other words you can use to let people know how you feel."

His mother's comments reminded Russell that he had been angry at Elisa. He picked up his little cars and took them away. Elisa began to cry.

"Aren't you going to share?" asked Mrs. Michaels.

"No," said Russell.

He was feeling angry all over again. His mother was telling him what words could come out of his mouth, and she wanted him to let Elisa play with his cars, too. He let Elisa play with them when she asked his permission. But he didn't like it when she just went to the box and took them out when he wasn't home.

That evening, while he was eating supper, a piece of meat flew off Russell's plate while he was cutting it.

Just as suddenly, the bad word flew out of Russell's mouth.

"KiKi doesn't like that word," said Elisa. KiKi was an imaginary friend that Elisa often spoke about. No one ever saw her, but Elisa insisted that KiKi was around most of the time.

"I don't care what KiKi says," Russell complained as he leaned down to pick up the meat from the floor.

"But I care what you say," said Mrs. Michaels. "Remember, I told you not to use that bad word."

"You never hear your mother or me saying it," Russell's father pointed out.

Russell looked at his food. He pushed the pieces of carrot and meat around on the plate with his fork. He didn't understand why saying a word could make his parents angry. Russell noticed that the more they complained about the word, the more he felt like saying it.

That night when he was in the bathtub, he made up a song about the word. He sang it to himself as he splashed in the water. But he didn't sing it out loud. He didn't want his parents to hear his bad-word song.

As he lay in bed, Russell thought about the word some more. He got out of bed and went into the living room. "I want a drink of water," he told his parents as he passed them on his way toward the kitchen.

Russell filled a glass with water at the sink. He carried it carefully into the living room so it wouldn't spill. "Is water a good or a bad word?" he asked.

"It's a good word, of course," said his mother, smiling. "Plants need water to grow. And people need water to drink and for washing."

"But if I spilled this glass of water on

the rug, you'd get angry," said Russell. "Then water would be bad."

"If *you* spilled the water, *you'd* be bad, not the water," said Mr. Michaels.

"But you aren't going to spill it," said Russell's mother. "You're going to finish your drink and then go right to bed. So we don't have to worry about whether water is a good word or a bad one."

"I'm not worrying," said Russell. "I'm just thinking."

"That's great," said his mother. "I'm glad you're thinking. You're such a smart boy, with so many 'Very Good' and 'Excellent' papers from school, that I'm sure you can think of plenty of good words to use when you talk. You don't have to use bad words."

"When I'm angry it feels good to say a

bad word," said Russell, taking a sip of water.

"Why don't you make up your own bad word?" said his father.

"How can I do that?"

"Make up a word that nobody else has. It can be a word that will mean *I am feeling angry,* but at the same time it won't be a word that will offend other people."

Russell smiled. That sounded like fun. He thought of words that he knew and sounds that he knew that weren't really words. "I could have a pretend bad word the way Elisa has a pretend friend," he said.

"Exactly," said his mother.

Russell leaned against the sofa and began whispering sounds to himself. His bad word would have to sound truly awful. That was important because it wasn't really going to be a bad word at all.

Mrs. Michaels turned a page of the magazine that she had been reading before Russell had gotten out of bed. "It's way past your bedtime," she told her son. "You can make up your word tomorrow."

She turned another page. It showed women wearing large hats.

"Hats. Schmatz!" said Russell.

"What?" asked his mother, looking up from her magazine.

"I just made up my word," Russell informed her. "Schmatz, schmatz, schmatz." It had a good strong sound to it, but it wasn't rude at all. Russell started to dance around the living room, calling out his bad word.

"Schmatz, schmatz, schmatz."

As he danced, he tripped over his father's foot. The glass of water, which he was still holding and which had been half full, spilled onto Mr. Michaels's pants leg, soaking it.

"Oh, Russell!" his father shouted in anger. "Now look what you have done."

Russell was sure his father was going to scold him. But instead, Mr. Michaels said the bad word. It wasn't a real bad word. It was the one Russell had invented. "Schmatz!" Mr. Michaels called out loudly.

Russell grinned with delight. His father liked the bad word he had made up, too.

"I'm sorry I got you wet," he said. He put the empty glass in the kitchen sink. Then he kissed his parents goodnight.

He was still whispering his new word

when he got back into bed. It was a good bad word. Russell knew he wasn't going to need any others.

"Schmatz!"

The Costume Party

It was almost Halloween. Nora and Teddy had been planning their costumes for weeks. Russell knew what he was going to wear when they all went out for trick or treat together. He had some pajamas that looked like a tiger's skin. Every year at Christmastime, he got a brand-new pair of tiger-skin pajamas from his aunt. Of course, each year they were a bigger size. He got so many toys for Christmas that he was never sorry to get pajamas in one of the boxes, especially such neat-looking ones. And every Halloween, he wore them for his costume.

"This year I'm going to be an astronaut," said Teddy.

"I'm going to be a gypsy," said Nora. "Are you going to be a tiger again?" she asked Russell.

"Yes." He nodded.

"Don't you get tired of always dressing up in the same costume?"

"No," said Russell. And it was true. He liked being a tiger.

The next day at school, Mrs. Evans made a surprise announcement. She said that on Halloween the children could all wear their costumes to school. There would be a parade all around the building and all the first-graders could show off their costumes to the other students.

"What are you going to be?" Jeremy asked Russell at lunchtime. "I'm going to be a cowboy."

"I'm going to be a tiger," said Russell. "I'm always a tiger. It's a good thing to be."

"You mean you're going to wear your tiger pajamas to school?" asked Jeremy. He had slept over at Russell's house just last weekend and he had seen Russell's pajamas then.

"Yes," said Russell.

"I never heard of anyone wearing their pajamas to school." Jeremy giggled.

"Are you really going to wear pajamas for Halloween?" asked a boy named Danny who was sitting with Russell and Jeremy at the lunch table.

Russell thought hard. He had always been a tiger. He liked being a tiger. But he didn't want people laughing because he was wearing his pajamas to school.

"No," said Russell. "I'm not wearing pajamas and I'm not going to be a tiger. I have a new costume."

"What is it?" asked Jeremy.

"It's a surprise."

"Is it a robot?" asked Danny.

"No."

"Is it a monster?" asked Jeremy.

"No."

"Tell me," Jeremy begged. "I told you what I'm going to be."

"I'll give you a piece of my cupcake," offered Danny.

Russell looked at Danny's cupcake. It had chocolate frosting. The cupcake looked so delicious that Russell would have told Danny all about his new costume. The only problem was that Russell didn't know what the costume would be. He turned his head so he didn't have to watch Danny licking the chocolate frosting.

"It's a surprise," Russell said. "You have to wait till Halloween to find out."

At home Russell asked his mother, "What can I dress up like for Halloween?" he wanted to know.

"Aren't you going to be a tiger?" his mother asked.

"I can't wear my pajamas to school," Russell complained. "I need a new costume."

Mrs. Michaels thought for a minute.

"Would you like to be a robot?" she asked. "I could help you make a costume out of boxes and aluminum foil."

Russell would have agreed to be a robot, but he remembered just in time that he had told Jeremy and Danny that he was not going to be one. "No," said Russell. "I have to be something different."

"A cowboy?" suggested his mother.

"Jeremy is going to be a cowboy," said Russell. "I can't be a cowboy, too."

"Sure you can," said his mother. She didn't understand that Jeremy would think that Russell had copied his idea.

"You could be a girl like me," offered Elisa. "I'll let you wear my best dress with russells." She meant ruffles, but she always got confused about that.

"I don't want to be a girl," said Russell.

"I'm afraid your dress would be too small for Russell," said Mrs. Michaels. "But it was very nice of you to offer."

"I'll ask Nora," said Russell. "She always has good ideas."

"You could be an astronaut like Teddy," offered Nora when she heard that Russell was not going to be a tiger this year, after all.

Russell shook his head.

"How about a monster?" said Nora.

"No," said Russell.

"Why don't you wear your tiger suit? You always do," said Teddy. "You're good at being a tiger."

"I can't wear pajamas to school," Russell explained.

"Don't tell anyone that they are pajamas," said Nora. "If you don't tell them, they won't know."

"But Jeremy already saw them when he slept over at my house. And I wore them when I went to sleep over at Alex's house. Everyone already knows that they are pajamas." Russell was feeling very angry with himself. Why hadn't he thought to wear his other pajamas, the ones with the polka dots, when he was with his friends?

Halloween was getting closer and closer, but Russell still couldn't think of an idea for a costume. *I'll just stay home from school,* he thought. *I'll pretend that I'm sick. I can't go to school if I am sick.* He didn't really want to stay home on Halloween. It would be fun to see everyone dressed in a costume. Even Mrs. Evans was going to wear one. And there was going to be ice cream and cake in the afternoon, too. But if he couldn't think of a good costume, Russell didn't want to go to school.

By the morning of Halloween, Russell still didn't know what to wear to school. He stood in his polka-dot pajamas and watched his father shaving by the bathroom mirror. His father didn't have any problem deciding what to wear to work. He wore the same kind of clothes every day. He wore shirts with long sleeves and a collar. He wore neckties and a jacket. He always looked very important.

"Well, how about it?" asked Mr. Michaels. "Are you going to be a tiger today, after all?"

"No," said Russell. "I want to be something special and I don't want to be an old tiger again."

Mr. Michaels buttoned his shirt and

began to put on his necktie. He looked in the mirror as he adjusted it.

"What do you want to be when you grow up?" he asked Russell. "It's too late now, but I guess that's the question we should have asked you. Then you could have dressed like a fireman or a policeman or whatever."

"I want to be a daddy like you," said Russell. And suddenly he had a wonderful idea. "Could I wear one of your neckties?" he asked.

His father laughed. "Sure," he said. He rushed to the bedroom. "Hurry and get dressed and I'll help you tie it," he said.

So Russell quickly removed his polka-dot pajamas. And instead of putting on his tiger pajamas, as he had done every Halloween for the past three years, he put on

slacks and a shirt and wore one of his father's neckties. Mr. Michaels found an old briefcase in the closet that he no longer used.

"Would you like to carry this today?" he asked.

"I could put my notebook and my papers in it," said Russell excitedly. "I will look very important, like a daddy."

"And here's a hat," said Mr. Michaels. He handed one of his old hats to Russell.

The hat was too big, but Russell didn't mind. He could hardly wait to go to school now. He looked in the mirror to admire his outfit. He noticed that the necktie that he was wearing had stripes that looked a little bit like his tiger stripes. *Wait till everyone sees me*, he thought. *Won't they be surprised.*

There were two cowboys, one Superman, one Mickey Mouse, three princesses, an astronaut, two gypsies, a robot, three monsters, three witches, two Martians, and one daddy in Russell's class that day. Mrs. Evans was dressed as a witch. But she told everyone that she was a good witch. The parade around the school was loads of fun and the food at the party in the afternoon was delicious. There was vanilla ice cream and cupcakes with chocolate frosting. There was candy, too.

Russell ate all of his cupcake and his ice cream, but he saved some of his candy to bring home for Elisa. That was the sort of thing a daddy would do.

At the Movies

One Saturday morning something wonderful happened. Russell was just getting
dressed when the telephone rang. It was
Mrs. Schuman, the mother of Carla
Schuman, who was in his class. Mrs.
Schuman told Russell's mother that she was
going to take Carla to the movies that
afternoon. She invited Russell to go, too.

When Russell heard that he had been invited to go to the movies with Carla, he was very excited. He seldom went to the movies. That was because Elisa was too young to sit through a whole film, and Mrs. Michaels couldn't take Russell to the movies without taking Elisa, of course. Sometimes Russell went with Nora and Teddy, but not often enough. At school the boys and girls in his class were always talking about movies that Russell had not seen. He liked it better when they discussed television programs. Then he could join in.

"Is it time to go yet?" Russell asked his mother about ten times that morning. He was in a hurry to go to the movie.

"Not until after lunch," his mother said. Russell hadn't even eaten his breakfast yet.

It was a long morning.

At last it was time for his mother to take him to Carla's house. Carla lived just a couple of blocks away, so they walked and Mrs. Michaels pushed Elisa in her stroller. "How much longer till Elisa will be able to go to movies?" Russell asked.

"Maybe in another year or two," said Russell's mother.

That seemed too far away for Russell even to imagine. But today he didn't care because he was going to the movies with Carla.

"We'll drop Russell off on our way home," Mrs. Schuman promised Mrs. Michaels.

Russell waved good-bye to his mother and Elisa.

"Have a good time," Mrs. Michaels

called as she and Elisa started the walk back home.

Russell and Carla smiled at each other shyly. They had only played together once before. In school Carla was very quiet and never spoke at all. Russell had thought that she didn't know how to talk. But when he had gone to her house to play last week, he was surprised that she could speak very well.

"My mother said we can have popcorn," Carla said as they walked toward the movie theater.

"Yummy!" said Russell. He loved popcorn. "Can we get soda, too?" Russell asked, turning to Carla's mother. "Popcorn makes me thirsty."

"We'll see," said Mrs. Schuman.

Russell nodded his head. He could tell

from the tone of her voice that they would get soda, too.

At the movie theater, Russell looked at all the pictures in the entranceway while Mrs. Schuman bought their tickets.

"Look at this!" he called to Carla. It was a picture of a huge fire and there were firemen rescuing people from a burning building.

"That's not a scene from the movie we are going to see," said Mrs. Schuman, looking at the picture, too. "This movie theater is a triplex. That means that it shows three movies at one time."

"How can you see so many movies at once?" asked Russell.

"You can't," Mrs. Schuman explained. "The theater is divided into three parts. We are going into the part that has the children's program. It's about a girl and her dog."

"I want to see the fire," said Russell.

"The fire is too scary," said Carla. She looked at the burning building one more time and then she covered her eyes.

"Come," said Mrs. Schuman. "Let's go inside and get our seats."

As they turned away, Russell looked back once more. He thought the fire looked very exciting. He wished he were going to see that movie.

Inside the theater, Mrs. Schuman bought a large container of popcorn. "I'll sit in the middle and hold this in my lap," she explained. "Then you will both be able to reach it and it won't spill."

Russell sighed. He wasn't going to see the fire movie and he didn't have his own box of popcorn. The afternoon wasn't turning out quite as well as he had hoped.

When they got to their seats, Russell saw many other boys and girls waiting for the movie to begin. Russell looked around to see if he could recognize anyone from school. Then the lights dimmed and the movie began. Even though there wasn't any fire in the movie they were watching, Russell liked the girl and her dog. The dog could do all sorts of tricks and whenever the girl was heading toward trouble, the dog would bark and warn her. Once the girl fell into a pond and the dog jumped right in and rescued her. He was a good dog, all right.

As he watched the film, Russell kept moving his hand in and out of the box of popcorn. It was a big box, and so even though Carla and her mother were sharing it, there seemed to be enough popcorn for all of them. It was a long time before Russell's hand hit the bottom of the container.

"Now will you get soda?" he whispered to Mrs. Schuman. Then he remembered to add, "Please."

"Do you mind if I leave you here a minute?" she asked.

"It's okay," said Russell.

"No," said Carla. "Take me with you. I have to go to the bathroom."

"Russell, are you sure you can sit here all alone?" asked Mrs. Schuman.

"Sure," said Russell.

"Maybe you should come with us."

"I don't want to go to the bathroom," said Russell. "And I don't want to miss the movie either."

"All right," Mrs. Schuman whispered. "We'll be right back."

Carla and her mother got up and walked up the aisle toward the door. Russell turned for a moment to watch them. Then he turned back to look at the screen. A man had caught the dog and put him in a big box.

Now that the dog was in the box, the movie wasn't so interesting. Russell liked it better when the dog was running around and doing his tricks. He watched for another couple of minutes, hoping that the dog would get out of the box. He didn't. Russell got thirstier and thirstier. He wished Mrs. Schuman and Carla would come back with the soda.

Then Russell remembered that he

had forgotten to tell Mrs. Schuman what flavor he liked best. Maybe she would get just one cup for them all to share. Maybe it wouldn't be orange, which was the flavor that he wanted.

Russell decided to get up from his seat and ask Mrs. Schuman to get orange soda. He left his jacket on his seat and walked to the exit door. He looked for Mrs. Schuman by the candy counter. He walked all around the lobby, but he couldn't see her. He decided that Mrs. Schuman and Carla must still be in the bathroom.

Russell wondered if the dog had gotten out of the box yet. He decided to go back into the movie. He opened the door and walked back inside the theater.

There was no dog on the screen, but there were several cars rushing someplace quickly. One of the cars crashed into the back of another. The first car spun around. Russell was fascinated. He sat down and wondered where the dog was. Maybe the dog was in a box inside the car.

Then he heard loud sirens. Fire engines were coming. The cars and the fire engines were all going in the same direction. It was another minute until they all reached the burning building. It looked a little like the apartment building where Russell lived. In fact, Russell thought it might be his building. Big flames were bursting out of some of the windows. There was the sound of breaking glass and a person jumped out of a window.

The firemen were putting up a ladder, but Russell was sure they were too late. He could see that some of the people would be burned. Maybe his mother and father and Elisa would get burned, too. Russell began to cry. He didn't want anything to happen to his family. And what about everyone else? Nora and Teddy and Mrs. Wurmbrand. Mrs. Wurmbrand was the oldest neighbor in the building. She couldn't run fast enough to escape from the fire.

"Russell, what are you doing in here?" said a voice in his ear.

Russell turned around. It was Mrs. Schuman.

"I was looking for you," he said.

"And I was looking for you," said Mrs. Schuman. Carla stood beside her mother with her hands over her eyes.

"Were you frightened?" asked Mrs. Schuman.

"No," lied Russell as the three of them walked out of the theater.

"You are crying," said Carla, peeking out from between her fingers now that they were safely away from the scene of the fire.

"No, I'm not," said Russell, sniffing hard.

"You shouldn't have gone into that movie," said Mrs. Schuman. "I told you it wasn't for children."

"I didn't know it was the wrong movie," said Russell. "When I couldn't find you, I guess I went back in through the wrong door."

"You certainly did," said Mrs. Schuman.

"I want to see my movie," said Carla.

"Come," said Mrs. Schuman, leading them through the correct doorway.

The dog was out of the box and

jumping all over the place. He was licking the girl's face and she was hugging him. Russell was glad that the dog was not burned in the fire. This was a much better movie than the one for grown-ups, he decided.

When the movie was over, they began walking toward Russell's house.

"My daddy said that someday I can have a dog," Carla said.

"I'm going to ask my daddy if I can have a dog, too," said Russell.

"Maybe I'll get two dogs," said Carla.

"Maybe I'll get three dogs," said Russell.

"Maybe I'll get four dogs," said Carla.

Russell was up to fifteen dogs by the time they reached his house. He was very relieved to see that there were no signs of a fire. He had known that it wasn't his house that was burning. Still, he felt better now that he could see for sure that all was the same as he had left it.

"I'm afraid we had a little bit of drama this afternoon," Mrs. Schuman apologized to Russell's mother. She explained what had happened when she took Carla to the bathroom.

"All's well that ends well," said Mrs. Michaels, giving Russell a hug.

Russell hugged her back. He was so glad that she wasn't burned in the fire.

It was only after Carla and her mother had gone home that Russell remembered something. He had never gotten any soda. Not orange or any other flavor.

The Report Card

One of the things that made first grade different from kindergarten was that in first grade the teacher sent a report card home to your parents. Russell had heard about report cards from Nora and Teddy. He had been very proud when he had gotten his report card for the first time in the fall. In the winter Russell had received his card with new marks on it. And now that it was spring, Mrs. Evans gave out the cards once again.

"Your parents will be eager to see your progress," she told the class. "Don't forget. After your parents read them, they should sign their names on the bottom line. Then return the cards to me, please."

Russell studied his yellow card. It was like a little folder and there were words written on all four sides. The first time he had seen his card, he could only read his name on it. But now he had become such a good reader that he was able to read almost all the words on the card. He was not surprised that Mrs. Evans had marked "Excellent" next to the boxes for Reading Readiness Skills and Manual Dexterity and Arithmetic Skills.

Russell knew that he was one of the best readers in the class. Already he had completed two workbooks and he had begun a third one. Some of the boys and girls in his class were still using the first workbook that Mrs. Evans had given them in September when they entered the class.

Once again Mrs. Evans reminded everyone that the boxes said "Excellent," "Good," "Fair," and "Needs Improvement." "I have checked the boxes that best describe each of you," she said.

Russell turned his card over. He saw that something was written on the back and the box was marked "Needs Improvement."

"What's back here?" Russell called out.

"On the back of the card, it tells about

your class behavior," Mrs. Evans explained. "Calling out without raising your hand is not good behavior."

Russell often called out. He couldn't help it. If he waited until Mrs. Evans noticed that his hand was in the air, it took too long. Sometimes Russell just had to shout out.

When Russell went home from school that day, he put his report card in his lunch box as Mrs. Evans had suggested. That way his mother would find the card and it wouldn't get lost.

Mrs. Michaels read her son's card. "Your father and I are proud of you. You are doing very good work," she told him. "I can hardly believe how much you have learned. And I'm sure your behavior will be getting better soon, too. Don't you think so?"

"Maybe," said Russell. He was a little angry that Mrs. Evans hadn't marked the "Good" box about that.

"I want another cookie," he said, finishing the two that his mother had given him, along with some milk, as an after-school snack.

"No more cookies now," said Mrs. Michaels. "You don't want to spoil your appetite for supper."

"Yes, I do," complained Russell. But Mrs. Michaels didn't give him any more.

After supper, Russell wanted to watch television. But his father wanted to watch a special news broadcast at the same time. Russell didn't care about news. It was too boring to watch men and women talking about things that he didn't understand.

"It's not fair that you get to watch what you want and I don't," said Russell.

"This is an important program," said Mr. Michaels. "Why don't you go play in your room so that I can see it in peace."

"I wish we had two television sets," he complained to his father.

"I wish you would keep quiet so that I can hear this program," Mr. Michaels responded.

"This is my home," said Russell angrily. "I can talk if I want to."

"You can go and talk in your bedroom!" shouted his father. "Go there right now. And stay there!"

Russell stormed out of the living room. He didn't care if he couldn't stay and watch television or talk to his father. He didn't want to talk to his father anyhow. His father was so mean to him.

Russell sat down on his bed to decide what he should do. From his room he could hear his mother giving Elisa her bath. His mother didn't care that he couldn't watch TV or talk with his father in the living room. Russell felt angry with his mother, too.

Then Russell got an idea. He would make a report card for his parents. He knew just which boxes he would mark. Russell went to his shelf and found a package of colored paper and a black marking pen.

Russell folded a sheet of yellow paper to make it look like his report card. Then he realized that he did not know how to spell important words like "Behavior." So, even though his father had ordered him to stay in his bedroom, Russell decided to tiptoe into the kitchen to get his report card. He could copy all the words he needed from it.

Elisa was talking in the bathtub as he walked past the open bathroom door. Russell decided she probably thought KiKi was in the bathtub, too. Mrs. Michaels didn't notice Russell and neither did Mr. Michaels, who was watching the television. In the kitchen Russell opened his lunch box, which was still on the counter, removed his report card, and tip-toed back into his room.

Then he began copying from the card:

REPORT CARD
Name: Mommy and Daddy

Even though he was angry at his parents tonight, Russell knew he had to mark the best box for Reading Readiness. They were both good readers and read lots of stories to him. Then he remembered that they weren't always *ready* to read a story whenever he wanted them to. Sometimes his mother said she had to finish cooking supper. Sometimes his father said he was too tired.

So Russell made a box and put a check inside. Underneath the box he wrote "Reading Readiness—Needs Improvement."

Russell looked at his report card. He didn't think it was so important to give his parents marks for Arithmetic Skills and Manual Dexterity. He decided to use his own words. He wanted to give

his parents marks in important things
like:

TV	Needs Improvement
Cookys	Needs ImpRovement
Presnts	NEEDS Improvement
Bed Time	Needs Improvement
Yelling	Needs Improvement

Russell covered all four sides of the
yellow paper. He drew a line at the
bottom so that his parents could sign
their names, just like they had to do on
his card. He listened hard and could
hear the water going down the drain
from the bathtub. He knew his mother
and Elisa would be coming into the
bedroom in another minute. Russell
hurried into the kitchen. He put his own

report card and the special one that he had made for his parents inside his lunch box. Wouldn't his mother be surprised when she opened it to put in his lunch for tomorrow?

The next morning, when Russell was having breakfast, his father said to him, "Russell, your mother and I received the report card that you made for us."

Russell looked up from his scrambled eggs. He had forgotten about the card in the night while he was sleeping.

"Did you see your marks?" Russell asked.

"Yes," said Mr. Michaels. "I'm sorry to say that we didn't get as good marks as you did."

"You should try harder," said Russell. This morning he did not feel angry at his father. He was a pretty good father, Russell thought. He wouldn't want to have a different one.

"I will try harder at home," said Russell's father, "if you will try harder at school."

"I try very hard at school," said Russell. "But sometimes I forget. I can't help it if I call out to Mrs. Evans."

"I know," said Mr. Michaels. "And I can't help it if I get impatient with you sometimes."

"Too many cookies would make you sick," said Mrs. Michaels to her son.

"A hundred cookies would make me sick," Russell agreed. "But three cookies wouldn't be too much for me. My stomach is much bigger now that I'm in first grade."

"All right," agreed his mother. "You try very hard to raise your hand in class and not to call out. And I'll have three cookies waiting for you when you come home today."

"Good," said Russell. It sounded like a fine plan.

"I've packed your lunch and your father and I both signed your report card. You have to return it to Mrs. Evans today," said Mrs. Michaels.

"And we've signed the other card, too. Do you want it back?" asked Russell's father.

"You can keep it," said Russell. "I can make another card if you need more improvement."

He put on his jacket to get ready for school. He grinned at his parents.

"Mostly you're pretty good," he said.

"Mostly you're pretty good, too," said Mr. Michaels, giving Russell a big hug before he went to work.

The Science Project

Russell liked science. He was learning all about it at school. Russell was happy to discover that dinosaurs were part of science. He had known about dinosaurs ever since he was as little as Elisa. He could identify pictures of the brontosaurus and the stegosaurus, the triceratops and the tyrannosaurus, because he had a book at home with pictures of them all.

But there were other kinds of science that Russell didn't know about at all. One week his class talked about stars. Russell learned that even though the stars looked teeny-tiny when he looked up at the sky at night, the stars were gigantic. They were bigger than his apartment building. They were even bigger than the whole city. It was hard to believe, but Mrs. Evans, his teacher, was so smart that if she said so, it must be true.

Another kind of science that the first-grade class learned about was *vitamins*. Even though vitamins were invisible so you couldn't see them, they were inside the food that Russell ate.

"Carrots have vitamin A," he announced proudly to his parents at dinnertime.

"Isn't it good that I cooked carrots for dinner tonight?" said Mrs. Michaels.

"KiKi doesn't like carrots," said Elisa. "She says vitamin A tastes bad."

"But you are smarter than KiKi," said her mother. "You know that you can't taste vitamins and that carrots are very good for you."

Elisa put a piece of carrot on her fork and raised it into her mouth.

"I think I can taste the vitamins a little bit," she said.

"You can't taste vitamins and you can't see them," Russell said. "I am learning everything about vitamins when we study science. Oranges and grapefruit and tomatoes have vitamin C," he told his family. "Potatoes have vitamin C, too."

Elisa lifted up her cup of milk and took

a drink. "Milk doesn't have any vitamins," she said. "Because if it did, the vitamins would get all wet."

"Yes, it does," shouted Russell. He had learned about milk, too. "Milk has vitamin D."

Elisa put down her cup and made a funny face. "I don't want to drink this milk," she complained.

"Elisa," said their father, "you can't see the vitamins and you can't smell the vitamins and you can't taste the vitamins. They are like magic."

Elisa smiled. Magic made more sense than vitamins. She put another carrot on her fork and ate it.

"You know something else," said Russell. "There is vitamin D in the sunshine, too. And you don't even have to eat it."

"How could you eat sunshine?" asked Elisa.

"You can't. You get vitamin D when you play outdoors in the sun."

"See," said Mr. Michaels. "It is just like magic."

"Vitamins are good for you. They help you grow big and strong," said Russell.

That night, when his parents kissed him goodnight, Russell had a question. "Do kisses have vitamins?" he asked.

Mr. Michaels laughed, but Mrs. Michaels said she was sure they did. "It's probably a letter that no one has discovered yet."

When the first grade completed the science unit about vitamins, Mrs. Evans announced that now they would learn about plants and how they grew.

"You will each grow your own plant as a science project," she informed the boys and girls. "There are many ways to grow plants right here in our classroom."

Russell learned that you could put a sweet potato in water and it would grow roots on the bottom and green stems and leaves on the top. You could bury grapefruit seeds in a pot with soil and green shoots would come up, but you wouldn't be able to see the roots because they would be under the dirt. For homework, each child was asked to bring a seed or a vegetable to school for planting.

Carla brought an avocado pit. Jeremy brought some beans. Two girls brought sweet potatoes, just as Mrs. Evans had mentioned the day before. But Russell wanted to be different. Besides, he liked regular potatoes better than sweet potatoes. He brought a big old potato that he had found in the cupboard. It had some funny bumps on it, and Mrs. Evans said they were called *eyes*.

"Can my potato see me?" asked Russell.

"These eyes can't see," Mrs. Evans explained. "But they are the way the potato will grow. Each eye is the beginning of a new potato plant."

In the classroom, there were many jars and pots for the first-graders to use to plant their vegetables. Mrs. Evans helped Russell cut his potato into four pieces. Then Russell buried the pieces in the soil. Russell got very dirty while he was doing it, so Mrs. Evans had to send him down the hall to the boys' room to wash up when he had finished.

"When will my potato grow?" Russell asked when he returned to the classroom.

"It will take time," Mrs. Evans said. "Plants grow faster than people. But still they grow too slowly for us to see."

The jars and the pots were set along the window ledge. During the day the sun shone in on them. Each day the children watered their plants. Russell was glad he hadn't planted a sweet potato. The sweet potatoes didn't need to be watered because they were already in water.

But Russell began to be very sorry that he hadn't planted beans like Jeremy. Jeremy's beans were growing fast. A tiny shoot came up in just a couple of days. No one else's plant had grown, but Jeremy's beans had a green stem that kept getting bigger.

"This is not a good science project," Russell called out.

"Raise your hand if you want to tell us something," Mrs. Evans reminded him.

Russell raised his hand and Mrs. Evans called on him.

"This is not a good science project," he said again.

"You already said that," said Jeremy.

Mrs. Evans ignored Jeremy. "You must be patient," she said. "You did not get to be as big as you are now in one week. It takes more than a week for a plant to grow, too."

"Then how come Jeremy's beans are growing already?"

"Some plants grow faster than others. Just like some people grow faster than others."

When it was spring recess, most of the plants had bits of green showing. The sweet potato plants had long white roots and tiny green shoots. Russell's potato plant had not grown at all.

Mrs. Evans told the first-graders that they would take their plants home over the vacation period. "School will be closed," she said. "So if you don't take them home, they will not be watered."

Russell did not want to take his plant home. It just looked like a pot of dirt. You couldn't tell that anything was underneath the soil.

"You carry it," he told his mother when she came to pick him up from school. "I hate that old potato plant."

"Maybe it will grow during the vacation," said Mrs. Michaels.

During the vacation period, Russell played with Jeremy and Carla. One day he went to the zoo with his parents and Elisa. He watered his potato plant once, but mostly he forgot all about it. Plants were not as interesting a kind of science as dinosaurs and stars and vitamins, he decided.

Then one morning during spring recess, his mother called to him as he was waking up. "Russell, come and look!" she shouted.

Russell went into the kitchen to see what his mother wanted.

"Look at your potato," she said. "It has sprouted."

Sure enough, there was a tiny little green stem sticking out of the soil.

"It grew! It grew! My potato really

grew!" Russell shouted. He danced around the kitchen with delight.

Now Russell could not wait to return to school and show off his newly sprouted potato plant. And the wonderful thing was that now that the growing had begun, his plant seemed to be a little bit bigger every day.

By the last day of vacation, there was a long green stem with several small green leaves on it. "Wait until Mrs. Evans sees this," he said proudly.

The next morning Russell ate his breakfast quickly and ran to brush his teeth. He left his potato plant on the kitchen table next to his knapsack and his lunch box.

When he came back into the kitchen, he saw something awful. Elisa had climbed up on one of the kitchen chairs to reach the plant. She stuck her hand into the pot and pulled the green stem out of the soil.

"My plant! My plant!" Russell screamed. "Elisa has ruined it. Schmatz. Schmatz."

Mrs. Michaels came running into the kitchen. "What's going on here?" she demanded.

"KiKi wanted to see the potatoes," Elisa explained.

"She ruined my science project," Russell wailed. He felt so furious that saying his bad word was not nearly enough. He picked up the pot and threw it down in anger. The pot landed with a thud and the dirt spilled all over the linoleum floor.

"Russell!" shouted his mother, grabbing Russell by the arm. "What did you do?"

"It's not my fault," shouted Russell. "It's Elisa's fault. She made me angry. She ruined my plant and now I don't have anything to take to school."

He looked down at the dirt all over the floor. He bent to pick up a lump of soil that was near his shoe. "Hey, look," he said as he held the lump in his hand. "This isn't dirt. It's a potato."

In his hand, Russell held a tiny baby potato. It was the size of a marble. He felt around in the dirt on the kitchen floor. He discovered two other tiny potatoes.

"Look what I grew!" he shouted with delight.

"You can show them to your class!" said Elisa, who had been silently watching.

So Russell took his three baby potatoes to show the first grade. No one else had a

real vegetable to show for their science project. Mrs. Evans kept the potatoes on display for a few days. Then she let Russell take them home.

His mother cooked them for him to eat. His science project sat on Russell's dinner plate. And even though he had learned that you can't taste vitamins, Russell was sure that at least this one time, he was able to taste the vitamin C in his potato. They were the best potatoes and the best vitamin C in the whole world.

Maybe it was from all the vitamins: A, B, C, D. When Russell's father measured Russell, the mark Mr. Michaels made on the closet door showed that Russell had grown more than an inch in the last few weeks. Russell hadn't seen himself growing. He hadn't felt it either. But just like the plants in the science project, Russell had sprouted.

And the next time that Mrs. Resnick brought some hand-me-downs from Teddy, the red slicker was in the box.

Russell hoped it would rain the next day so Carla and Jeremy and his other classmates could see him standing tall in the red coat. In fact, he decided, he would wear the slicker tomorrow, even if the sun was shining.